Ross Burach

Scholastic Inc.

¡OYE!
¿Qué estás haciendo?

Polinizando.

¿Polini... QUÉ?
Llevando el polen de una flor a otra.
Obvio.
¿Por qué?

A TRABEJAR
Tiempo = ¡MIEL!
Miel=mc²
Abejeinstein
Las flores usan el polen para producir semillas.
Semilla
Las palabras del día:
Polinizar
Ecosistema
Semilla
Las semillas se convierten en plantas que producen más flores y frutos.
Todo eso ayuda a mantener el ecosistema.
ABEJA
Nada del otro mundo.
Semilla → fruta → comida

P.M.I.
POLINIZADOR MUY IMPORTANTE
NOMBRE: Abeja
Ayudante del ecosistema

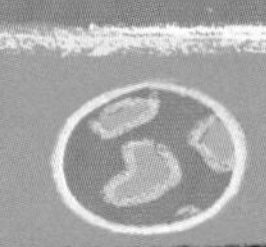

¡VAYA! Ojalá yo fuera un polinizador muy importante.

¡Lo eres!

Claro. Claro.
Ya lo sabía.

Un momento... ¿Quieres decir que soy un POLINIZADOR?

Sí.

¿Y que ayudo a las flores a crear NUEVAS FLORES?

Sí.

¿Ahora qué?

Cómete el néctar y
deja que se te pegue el polen.

Claro. Claro. El polen.
Y ¿qué era el polen?

Esos granos amarillos.

ATENCIÓN, ECOSISTEMA...
¡Voy a recolectar
MÁS POLEN QUE NADIE!

¿QUEEÉ?

¿¿¿Cómo recolectaste TANTO POLEN???

¡Tengo pelitos por TODO EL CUERPO!

¡Ay! Yo no soy tan pegajosa.

No importa. No tienes que recolectar tanto polen como una abeja. Sé una mariposa.

Claro. Claro.
Quieres decir que debo ser **MÁS PEGAJOSA.**
PEGAMENTO SÚPER DÚPER PEGAJOSO SECA RÁPIDO
aprieta
PEGAMENTO en barra

Ay, no. Demasiado pegajosa.
No puedo moverme.

Tengo una pregunta.

¿Sí?

No es para mí. Es para un amigo.

Ya. ¿Cuál es la pregunta?

Digamos que un amigo
se quedó pegado a una flor.
¿Qué consejo le darías?

¿Qué estás haciendo AHORA?

Llenando mis canastas de polen para cargar más polen.

¿Yo tengo eso?

No. Tú no tienes que cargar tanto polen como una abeja. SOLO sé una mariposa.

Claro. Claro. Quieres decir que necesito mis propias canastas de polen.

¿Estás segura de que puedes volar cargando tanto polen?

Por supuesto. Las mariposas podemos cargar CINCUENTA VECES nuestro peso.

Pensaba que esas eran las hormigas.

¡PLAM!

Son las
hormigas.

¿Y ahora qué?
Volamos de flor en flor y comemos más néctar.
FIUM
CHUPA
CHUPA
CHUPA
AGUA
El polen cae y las flores hacen el resto.
FIUM
Ya. Y... ¿¿cuántas flores visita una abeja a diario??
Unas 3000.
FIUM

¡¿3000 flores?!
¡No puedo volar tan rápido!
Soy más de aletear.

¡Una mochila cohete!

Ecosistema, no temas...
¡AQUÍ ESTÁ EL POLINIZADOR!

¡ABRAN PASO A LA MARIPOSA!
EL POLINIZADOR
EL POLINIZADOR
EL POLINIZADOR
FPH 1000

¡CRAS!
ZADOR
¡Ay! No sirvo
como mariposa.

Eso es. Tengo que parecerme MÁS a Abeja.
PARTES de una ABEJA
Rayas
PELO
CANASTA

Tengo que ser más peluda.
POM-PONES

Y más zumbona.
BZZZ
BZZZ
BZZZ
Bzzz
BZZZ
BZZZ

Y más rayada.
Dibuja
Dibuja
Dibuja

Y más pegajosa.
PEGAMENTO en barra

Y más aguijonuda.

¡Siempre es bueno tener más canastas de polen!
MOSKEA
canasta

AHORA soy un Polinizador Muy Importante.
BZZZ
BZZZ
BZZZ
BZZZ

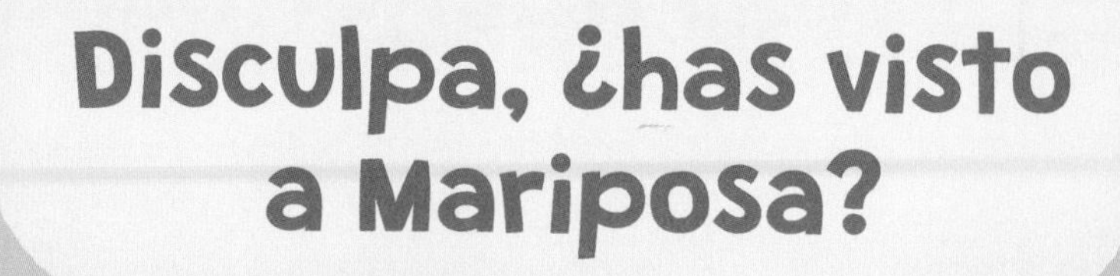

No. Aquí solo hay abejas. ¡BZZZ, BZZZ, BZZZ!

Qué pena. Tengo una labor importante para una mariposa.

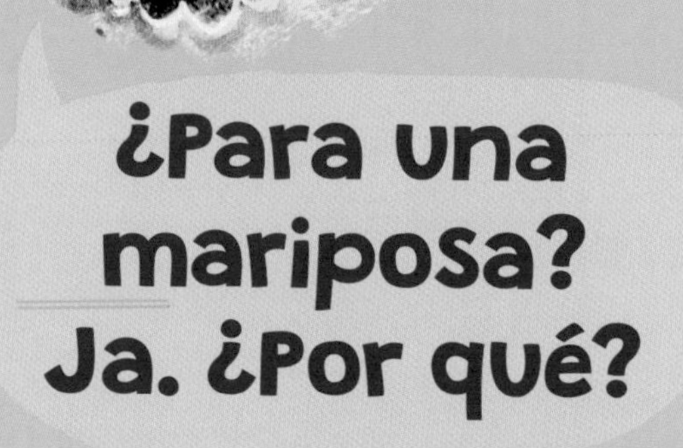

HOGAR Dulce NIDO
Como sabes, las abejas debemos estar CERCA de nuestro nido.
Si TAN SOLO hubiera aquí una MARIPOSA que llevara el polen a las flores lejanas.

¡Abeja! ¡Soy yo! ¡Mariposa!

¡Puedo ayudar! Puedo volar grandes distancias.

¡TÚ puedes!
CHUPA
CHUPA
CHUPA

Sé una mariposa,
sé una mariposa.

¡Lo logré! ¡Ayudé al ecosistema!

¿Viste? Nuestras diferentes maneras de polinizar son ambas **MUY IMPORTANTES.**

¡Tienes razón! ¡A partir de ahora haré todo lo posible por ser una mejor **MARIPOSA!**

BOMBILLO

O tal vez una luciérnaga...
Ay, no.

A Polly

Originally published in English as *Make Way for Butterfly*

Translated by Abel Berriz

 · ISBN 978-1-338-89675-6 · 10 9 8 7 6 5 4 3 2 1 23 24 25 26 27 · Printed in the U.S.A. 40

Ross Burach's art was created with pencil, crayon, acrylic paint, and digital coloring. · The text type was set in Grandstander Classic Bold. · The display type was set in Grandstander Classic Bold. Production was overseen by Jessie Bowman. · Manufacturing was supervised by Katie Wurtzel.
The book was art directed and designed by Marijka Kostiw and edited by Tracy Mack. Spanish translation edited by María Domínguez.